I'm a New Big Sister

ISBN: 978-1-60169-009-8

Published by innovativeKids®
A division of innovative USA®, Inc.
18 Ann Street
Norwalk, CT 06854
iKids is a registered trademark in Canada and Australia.

www.innovativekids.com

Printed in China
3 5 7 9 10 8 6 4 2

I'm a new big sister!

Mom and Dad say things will be a little different now.

I want to play with you, but for now you just watch me and smile.

Mom says someday you will be big like me, and we will play together.

I try to pick up all my toys.

Dad says it's important so that you don't get hurt.

I like when Mom and Dad let me help. I am very careful with you.

I hold you gently.

I read to you.

I push you in the stroller.

I help wash you in the bath.

I even help feed you when you're hungry.

I try not to get peas on your face.

Mom says someday you'll eat all by yourself from a plate, just like me.

Uh oh! I smell something stinky.
I think it's time for a new diaper.

I make funny faces so you don't cry when Dad changes you.

Sometimes you cry really loudly! Mom says babies cry when they need something.

Mom sits with you in the rocking chair, and we sing you a lullaby. That's just what you needed!

When you go to sleep, I spend time with Mom and Dad.

We read books.

We play games.

And we talk and laugh until our bellies hurt!

When it's time for me to go to bed, I put on my pajamas and brush my teeth all by myself.

Mom and Dad are very proud of me. They tuck me in tightly and kiss me goodnight.

Wow, things sure are different around here . . .

. . . they're even better now that I'm a new big sister!

Our Family

A Note to Parents

Congratulations! A new baby in the family is a wonderful milestone. But for big sister, it can be a time of uncertainty. By taking the time to talk to your daughter and understand her feelings, she will soon share in the excitement of the new baby.

Here are a few ideas to help big sister adjust to having a new baby in the family.

- Include big sister as much as possible! It is completely normal for big sister to question her place in the family and wonder and worry about life with the new baby. By inviting her to help and by including her in your conversations and activities, she will be more eager to join in with the new baby, and she will feel happy and loved. Whether she gets a towel for you at bath time or she helps to open a door, making her feel needed and valued will help her accept the new baby and feel good about herself.

- Constantly remind your child of how special she is! Use concrete examples to show her that you notice and appreciate her. Tell your daughter that you like the way she cleaned up her toys or that you like the picture she made. You can even write her little notes to remind her that you love her.

- Set aside time devoted to big sister! Carving out even 10 minutes a day when you and your daughter have quality time together can make all the difference. Spending time with only you will show big sister how important she is to you, and you will also cherish that special one-on-one time. You can simply read a book together, play a board game, or go outside and play catch. It is also fun to plan an outing for just the two of you—like to the ice cream shop or to the park!

- Try to keep as many of your old routines as possible! While you are all experiencing many changes, your daughter needs some consistency in order to feel safe and at home. Try your best to maintain the routines you had before the new baby arrived. Familiar routines will be a welcome part of an otherwise unpredictable day.

Just remember to take it one day at a time, share lots of laughs and tickle parties, and give lots of hugs and snuggles!

Now that you're a new big sister...

Be on the lookout for many exciting baby milestones!

In the first month, watch for baby to make sucking motions with his mouth. This probably means that baby is hungry.

Get ready to hear baby coo and gurgle in month two. The more you talk and sing to baby, the more language he will develop.

Smile! Baby will begin to recognize your face by month three. Get face to face with baby, and let him see you up close. Very soon, he will also start to smile!

In month four, baby may try reaching for a toy. Try putting a safe toy near baby, and see if he tries to reach for it!

Slow and steady! Baby may start to roll over from his tummy to his back in month five!

Try this in months six and seven: see if baby can imitate the sounds you make, and watch for baby to sit without support.

Eating is an adventure around month eight. Look for baby to start picking up finger food.

Ready for takeoff! By month nine, baby may be starting to crawl. Encourage baby to crawl by sitting across the room and calling him toward you.